C000108445

THE NORTH STAR

Martin Mellett was born in 1973, in Coventry, West Midlands. He graduated in 1999 from Coventry University with a degree in European Business Studies (spending one year at IUT de Saint-Étienne as part of the Erasmus programme) and went on to get a Certificate of Education (CertEd) at the University of Warwick, subsequently teaching adults English, Mathematics and Digital Skills. He is the youngest of three siblings, son of a motor mechanic and carer, and author of two novellas (*The North Star* and *Bob and the Universe*). His love of Chinese martial arts meant he became a master of T'ai Chi. He also regularly attends Extinction Rebellion meetings and demos.

To Will

Best Wishes

From

Martin

'The state of the planet is broken. Humanity is waging war on nature. This is suicidal. Nature always strikes back and it is already doing so with growing force and fury.'

António Guterres, Secretary-General of the United Nations

'The fact is that no species has ever had such wholesale control over everything on Earth, living or dead, as we now have. That lays upon us, whether we like it or not, an awesome responsibility. In our hands now lies not only our own future, but that of all other living creatures with whom we share the Earth.'

Sir David Attenborough, *Life on Earth*

'We could have saved ourselves, but we didn't. It's amazing. What state of mind were we in to face extinction and simply shrug it off?'

Pete Postlethwaite, *The Age of Stupid*

'With global warming things are different. I feel now that we only have two seasons. Winter turns directly into summer without us noticing.'

Fernand Pareau, Mountain Guide in France's Chamonix Valley

'We can no longer let the people in power decide what is politically possible.'

Greta Thunberg, *Youth4Climate* summit

'Glaciers melting is a signal that the Earth is destabilizing and all the norms that have allowed life to exist as it has done are changing.'

Piers Guy, Wind Turbine Builder

'*The North Star* is an exhilarating read that leaves the reader pondering today's problems on a personal and societal level.'

Positive Images Festival

'I can only quote George Monbiot in his recent article, Willing the End: It's as if, when ministers go to bed, they ask themselves, "What have I done to make the UK a worse place today?" *The North Star* delights in its plainness and devours in its subtle attack on the idiotic era we now live in.'

Ade Kolade, ex-researcher at The University of Manchester

'We put mediocre, comedy robots in charge of the country promising to "unleash" and "deliver". Well, pretty soon there'll be nothing *to* deliver. We'll all have been washed away. *The North Star*, to its credit, takes us back to a better time, a simpler time, highlighting the justified chants and actions of Extinction Rebellion, as well as walking us through a tale of one man's redemption.'

Andrew Routledge

'A gentle and moving exploration of two people navigating life before and during the Covid-19 pandemic. *The North Star* is steeped in references to Coventry; the local allotment, pub and poetry group scenes familiar to everyone. Martin has created characters that are relatable and who readers will undoubtedly feel a huge fondness towards.'

Emilie Lauren Jones, Coventry Poet Laureate

'Paul Kingsnorth in Apocalypse Soon writes of there being "no escape... from the [global economy's] products, its worldview or its 15G connectivity". It is a prescient essay with a dystopian tinge. Unfortunately, power attracts 'Yes' men (and women) and ruinous bastards and so it was rather inevitable that Planet Earth would one day resemble a trash can. Mellett isn't Caroline Lucas, Asad Rehman, Hugh Fearnley-Whittingstall or indeed, Kevin Anderson, but he is someone who cares deeply and such empathy is at the heart of the beautiful, slow novella that is *The North Star*.'

Jeff Weston, author of *Wagenknecht*

Martin Mellett

THE

NORTH

STAR

THINKWELL BOOKS

Copyright © 2022 Martin Mellett.

All rights reserved. No part of this publication may be reproduced, distributed, or transmitted in any form or by any means, including photocopying, recording, or other electronic or mechanical methods, without the prior written permission of the publisher, except in the case of brief quotations embodied in critical reviews and certain other noncommercial uses permitted by copyright law. For permission requests, contact the publisher.

Any references to historical events, real people, or real places are used fictitiously. Names, characters, and places are products of the author's imagination.

Edited by Jeff Weston.

Proofread by Anne Woodford.

Interior formatting by Rachel Bostwick.

Published by Thinkwell Books, U.K.

First printing edition 2022.

For my mum

"Love is like the North Star.
In a changing world, it is always constant."
- Gordon B Hinckley

CONTENTS

FOREWORD

Contrary to public perception, or portrayal in the mainstream media, the lives of those of us in Extinction Rebellion are just as ordinary as yours. Our actions can result in detention/imprisonment, fines and great personal cost, emotionally, socially and professionally, yet the realities of our lives are ever-present. Children are born, our elders deteriorate and die, and we go through all the ups and downs in between. I can't help but feel that we must urgently express unbounded gratitude for life itself.

Generation upon generation have failed to act in rational response to the scientific understanding that carbon emissions will trap heat in our atmosphere and acidify our oceans. As I write this we are firmly on course for collapse. We have been able to live with this knowledge and perpetuate systems of rampant extraction, exploitation and destruction, ignorant of the fact that structural endemic violence of this nature, scaled to the global level, will inevitably lead to a form of self-destruction. A wise man once said if you develop the power of gods you better hope that you can develop the wisdom of gods. I believe that to speed up our wisdom we need to listen more.

I sometimes find reassurance in the thought that from this point onwards, no matter what we do, the society we have built and are used to is over. It will either be transformed beyond recognition, or it will break down around us. This is hopefully an opportunity for us to let go of what we've known, and to redesign everything. I've often said that our rebellion is made of love. I have also often said that our rebellion is made of art - that choosing to make embodied resistance your priority in these times is the equivalent of turning your life into some sort of work of art. There is also an art to listening, noticing and recognising our real longings. What are we living for? Whilst we concern ourselves so greatly with scientific data, carbon emissions, species loss, cold analysis, do we lose sight of our love of the simple things in life?

We want to move forward with more of us having a say in shaping our future, because the majority of people mostly care for the simple things, like Jim. Jim originally chased money. He took drugs to escape reality. He sought status in the city. But in the end he's happier with his hands in the dirt, feeling close to his family - finally paying attention to his father's life's work, with his arms around someone who's showed him compassion and care. Illness and death called to tell him to stop what he was doing and shift his primary purpose to one of care, and with that time and focus he truly became himself.

The situation we find ourselves in can seem overwhelmingly complex, but our principal solution has always been remarkably simple: Work hard at better dialogue; Reweave the damaged fabric of our relations; Create the possibility of different decisions by making the conditions for 'change to take place'.

Love is the bedrock of the wisdom we need if we are to succeed in saving humanity.

Clare Farrell (co-founder of Extinction Rebellion), 18 August 2022

Spring

Chapter 1 - The Plough

Jim stood staring up at the night sky. He had found the Plough and was searching for the North Star. There it is, he thought, not very bright but definitely the North Star. It was like a small glimmer of hope in the darkness. Jim's dad was very much into astrology and used to tell him about it when he had been a child, pointing out the different stars and constellations. Jim was fascinated at first but soon lost interest, as with most things his dad introduced him to.

Jim had just been to a local pub where his dad used to go. Funnily enough, it was called The Plough. He had had two pints of beer and sat near the bar, half watching a Premiership football match on the big screen. He felt downhearted as he sipped his beer slowly, feeling very alone in the world.

He had decided to take the short cut back home, through the park as he used to when he first started going out at night many years ago. It was a cold, clear night with almost a January full moon; a wolf moon if he remembered his dad correctly. It glistened on the flowing river as he walked along and helped him see where he was going.

He walked past the big oak tree that stood beside the River Sherbourne heading into town. It had a huge trunk with branches stretching out wide. It must be very old, thought Jim. It's like the mother of the park.

He heard the river gently flowing by and could vaguely see a rope still hanging from one of the tree's long, thick branches with a small piece of wood attached horizontally at the bottom. Some things will never change, Jim thought, as he remembered jumping off the edge of the river bank as a youngster - his hands tightly gripping the wood, as if he could do anything he wanted in the world.

He looked up at the night sky just before leaving the park, locating the Plough and then the North Star again. He looked at it for a while before nodding his head, as if saying goodnight, and then walked onto the pavement and towards home.

~ ~ ~

Jim's dad had not long passed away. He'd had a stroke six months ago and Jim had moved home to Coventry from London to look after him. His dad was a private man and didn't want people coming into the house looking after him. So, Jim did all he could, making life as pleasant as possible for him. He couldn't walk unaided but Jim used to take him out to the shops in his wheelchair and sometimes on a Sunday afternoon to The Plough for a drink.

Jim's mum had had Alzheimer's and died ten years ago. His dad gave up everything and became her full-time carer, not putting her into a home as many professionals had recommended. He looked after her diligently making sure she had everything that she needed. Jim came back from London the odd weekend and was astonished at how well his dad was doing looking after her. He would still make her laugh and have fun with her even when she started to deteriorate. His dad had just taken hold of the reins as her carer and accepted it.

Although Jim didn't think he shared the same interests as his dad, he had seen a side to him in the last six months that he hadn't known before. Jim became interested in what his dad was going on about for the first time in the fifty three years that he'd known him. "The world is changing and we've got to do something about it!"

Jim began looking through some of the old magazines that his dad had kept over the years in the loft, about the environment and saving the planet. He got them down, brushed off the dust and started reading them to find out what his dad had been going on about. They were about greenhouse gases mainly, coming from fossil fuels, and how we needed a mass move to renewable energy. If we continue with fossil fuels, they said temperatures will continue to rise. Warming above 1.5 degrees Celsius risks further sea level rises, extreme weather, biodiversity loss and species extinction, as well as food scarcity, worsening health and poverty for millions of people worldwide.

Jim also read in the magazines about factory farming and how it uses greenhouse gases throughout the supply chain. For example, forest clearance to grow crops and rear animals reduces vital carbon and releases gases previously stored in the soil and vegetation. Factory farming also requires large amounts of energy in order to function. This isn't just to rear the animals, but also to grow the vast amount of feed they need. Jim couldn't believe the enormity of the problem and began to realise what his dad had been saying and how it should be on the front page of every newspaper.

It was just a couple of weeks since Jim's dad's funeral and he was shattered, physically and mentally, after sorting everything out single-handedly. He'd invited his dad's friends to the funeral, which was bigger than he imagined it would be. People travelled from different parts of the country to be there; his dad had been quite popular in his field of work as a university lecturer in Environmental Science. People said things to Jim at the reception afterwards that he wasn't aware of, for example his dad's active role in campaigns for the environment and protecting biodiversity.

Jim still had his flat in London although he hadn't been there for a while. He'd been working as a stockbroker in the city for many years up until a year ago when he had to stop work due to ill health. He was a workaholic and would work way too many hours each week, and weekends too meeting clients, and had simply burned himself out. He had no wife and no kids to look after, so his work was his life. He'd even lost interest in his football club due to his work commitments. He was like a car with the engine always running and his lights on full beam.

Jim had been thinking of selling his flat in London and returning permanently to his hometown before his dad died. He'd had enough of the rat race in London where everything revolved around money - what you had, where you lived, what you wore and where you went on holiday. Jim knew from how he was brought up that there was more to life; putting your energy and passion into something you felt strongly about was what mattered. The problem was there wasn't something like this in Jim's life.

He had been out of work for a few months before his dad had the stroke. He just had to stop as he knew he was heading for a breakdown. He'd seen it before with some of his colleagues and he recognised the signs: getting irritable over nothing, and not being able to switch off from work, thinking about it all the time.

He would always speak to his dad on the phone at weekends to see how he was doing, but he didn't tell him about being out of work as he knew he would be worried. They would chat about the usual things, what his dad was growing in his allotment, how the weather was changing, that he was planting things at different times of the year and was worried about how they would grow in the future. The conversations were virtually one way with his dad speaking most of the time. But Jim didn't mind, as he felt good after hearing a familiar voice, and his dad was a constant in talking about something he believed in.

Jim didn't know what to do with his life. He couldn't go back to working in the city and didn't have a clue what other job he could do. Money wasn't a problem for him as he'd made a lot over the years. So he spent most of his days doing the Guardian cryptic crossword and reading books.

It was Jim's mum that got him into reading at an early age. She was an English teacher at a secondary school and loved books and was determined to pass this gift onto her only child. Jim was a quick learner and was talking at an early age and soon reading as well and was way ahead of his peers. He would read the books at school with the other children but once home his mum would stretch him by giving him more advanced books.

Jim intended to go straight up to look after his dad as soon as he got news that he'd had a stroke. He told his dad he could look after him as he was having a break from working in the city. In a way, it was a godsend for Jim, as it gave him a purpose just as he was drifting and going nowhere. There was no one else to look after his dad and he fitted into the role of carer; he just did what needed to be done.

Jim's dad left the hospital after four weeks, but couldn't walk. He received physio at home, improved and could then walk a little. His speech was only slightly affected, but Jim noticed he got better after talking to him; so, he would talk with him every day, usually about the environment and climate change. He told Jim how to deal with his allotment, like making sure the carrots were thinned out and the weeds weren't getting the better of his plot that was beside the park, not far from the house. Jim's dad adapted to his new role as the boss, Jim thought, as he smiled inwardly going off to the allotment most days with his list of instructions.

Jim and his dad were getting on well - better, in fact, than ever before. His dad seemed to know that Jim was changing, realising that money wasn't everything and was seeking out a new life for himself. They were becoming more like friends than father and son. It was a massive shock therefore when his dad got pneumonia, went into hospital and died shortly afterwards. He had been eating well, as he always did, using vegetables that Jim dug up, cleaned and cooked for him. Jim had thought he was recovering well from the stroke. He was walking more and even went to The Plough on Sundays and to the allotment with Jim to see how his vegetables were getting on. So, Jim was devastated.

Jim carried on going to the allotment each day after the funeral, not really knowing what to do other than follow the instructions that his dad had given him. Spring was just coming, the birds were chirping, and people were getting busy turning the soil and planting seeds. It was a time of new beginnings, but Jim didn't feel such hope. He had just lost his dad, had no job and didn't know what he was going to do with the rest of life.

Then he met Geraldine who also had an allotment and knew his dad well.

Chapter 2 - Geraldine

There was a main shed at the allotment which was open on Saturday mornings that sold seeds, onion sets and potatoes for growing. They had all types of potatoes from first earlies to lates. Jim met a lot of people there, some familiar faces and others that were new to him. His dad had been on the allotment's committee, so he thought a few might know him. There were all ages of people at the allotment, from young families to elderly people, some who had had an allotment for years. One elderly couple, who he faintly remembered from when he came down here with his dad as a child, would always smile at him and say hello.

Jim noticed that there was a big congregation of birds at the allotment now that spring was on its way. They were happy singing in the trees and seemed to like people getting busy on their plots, digging up the soil (with worms appearing) and putting the compost down.

Jim had read up on the internet about the best things to grow this time of year and talked to some of the older men at the allotment who had a fountain of knowledge of what grew well in the soil and the best time to sow. He'd also found out about planting with the moon cycles.

While Jim was at the allotment, he didn't think about anything else and felt much more relaxed when he came back home. He thought he could have done with an allotment when he was feeling depressed after leaving his job in London.

Then one bright day in the middle of January, Jim was at the allotment digging the soil up, getting it ready for sowing seeds, when he noticed a woman looking at him over the gate to his plot, which he had recently officially taken over. He thought it only polite to go over and introduce himself.

"Hi, my name's Jim. I've taken over the plot from my dad who recently passed away. You may have known him. His name was Andrew McClean."

"Oh yes, I knew Andrew very well. I've had an allotment here for a long time too. There's a few of us die-hards still around who have been planting seeds for years. My name's Geraldine. Pleased to meet you," she said, as she offered out her hand to Jim.

Jim shook hands with her and noticed what a strong grip she had. She looked younger close up, with eyes that were very much alive and in the moment. Her hair was long and grey and tied back so it wouldn't get in the way of her working. She was quite small, although her arms looked strong, and she had a ring through her nose. A dog was sitting obediently beside her without a lead on.

Geraldine had a good aura about her that certain people have, and Jim liked her immediately. They got talking and Jim poured out his situation to her - how he didn't know what to do with his life, but liked coming to the allotment. It was quite strange as Jim wasn't normally like this and usually kept himself to himself. Geraldine was silent, just nodding occasionally and constantly keeping eye contact with him while taking in each word.

"Well, you've come to the right place," Geraldine laughed, when Jim was finished.

Jim laughed too as he put his hand on the spade which was dug deep into the soil beside him.

"My allotment is on the other side, but you'll see me walking my dog Theo around here. I like seeing people working on their plots and the scents they give off at different times of the year. There's a new meadow in the park which is good for the bees and it attracts all sorts of insects and birds. You should pop over some time."

"Yes, I saw that it was new to the park. Things have changed a bit since I was living here."

"We need to do more though if we're going to make a difference."

"You're right, if we all did our bit..."

Jim smiled as he thought he must sound like his dad, and Geraldine smiled too as if she knew what he was thinking.

"I belong to the local group of Extinction Rebellion," said Geraldine, "and we've got a meeting tomorrow night. Why don't you come along? You'll meet some interesting people."

"OK, I will," said Jim without thinking.

"I'll pick you up just before eight then. I know where you live," she said, as she turned around with her dog and walked off towards the meadow.

Jim had hardly heard of Extinction Rebellion and didn't know what it stood for. But I'll go, he thought, as he took hold of his spade with two hands and began digging again.

~ ~ ~

Jim got talking to Geraldine as soon as he got into her car. She had beeped the horn outside, but he was ready, with his jacket on and his keys in his pocket.

"What do you know about HS2?" asked Jim. "My dad was concerned about it and was saying it shouldn't go ahead."

"No, it shouldn't. Some of my friends are camping at one of the places where they are cutting down trees in the woodland in Buckinghamshire that inspired Roald Dahl. I've been to see them and go to the demos at the nearby line in Crackley Wood as well."

"It sounds like they're just cutting through the countryside to get the job done."

"Exactly. That's why it should never have gone ahead."

They shortly arrived at the local pub which wasn't too far from Jim's house. They got some drinks in and sat down with the other members and started talking straight away.

Jim liked the people at the meeting. They were of different age groups and were there for what they believed in. They were enthusiastic, but weren't there for themselves - instead looking at the bigger picture and future generations.

Jim had never been to something like this before and thought that he must stand out. But the group simply accepted him for who he was and asked no questions about his background or what he was doing. They all contributed and listened very attentively to what others had to say and even asked Jim what he thought about issues they were raising such as ideas for a campaign to highlight the urgency of the climate crisis.

"I hope you enjoyed the meeting," said Geraldine, as they got back into her car afterwards.

"I did," said Jim.

"Great. We'll see you at the next one then?" she smiled, as she put her key into the ignition.

"You will indeed." Jim also smiled as she drove him home.

Chapter 3 – Sowing the Seeds

Jim had put his flat up for sale in London and was moving back to his hometown permanently. It felt like the right thing to do. He had made some friends in London but had lost contact with them over the past year due to him leaving his job and then moving back home to look after his dad. The people he was meeting now were different and not so interested in money.

In other ways, Jim thought that he was going backwards in life. He had had an exciting time living in London, mixing with wealthy people and going out to expensive restaurants and having holidays abroad. He was now back where he started, living in the house where he was brought up.

He put most of his furniture into storage and moved the rest of his stuff into the back room where his dad had some of his folders and information on environmental issues. His dad wasn't one for getting rid of things or having a clear out and would always say that somebody might need them one day.

Jim had cleaned the greenhouse in the garden last year when he moved back and so it was ready for planting new things. It had been there for as long as Jim could remember. The allotment was just behind the garden, so it wasn't too far to go with the young seedlings when they were ready for planting. Jim had planted some seeds in small pots and was watering them regularly. He remembered his dad doing this each morning before going to the university where he lectured, and again in the evenings making sure they were all OK and well watered. He was determined to get them ready for planting out in his allotment. Jim used to sometimes think his dad paid more attention to his vegetables than he did anything else.

It was the end of January and the days were just starting to get longer. It had been very mild with temperatures above average. Jim always liked this time of year, even while living in the hustle and bustle of London. The birds singing each morning reminded him of his dad's allotment and how Jim's dad always knew the birds by sound or sight.

"You're like an encyclopedia," Jim's mum would say.

She used to walk down to him at the allotment, carrying baby Jim on her back, with sandwiches for the two of them. They would sit on a bench and she'd put a rug down for Jim to crawl around on. They'd have a flask of tea and sit and chat and watch Jim who seemed to be fascinated by the place with all the insects, bees and birds. He would then curl up and fall asleep, and Jim's mum would get out her book and read while his dad carried on working on the allotment.

There were still parsnips and leeks in the plot from last year. Jim ruefully dug them up knowing that these would be the last ones his dad had planted. He carefully took them out of the soil, making sure none of them broke off. There's an art to this, he thought, as he put them in the old wheelbarrow that had been there as long as he could remember. He then walked up to the gate where Geraldine was standing, watching with her dog, Theo.

"That's a good load you've got there," she said.

"Sure is," Jim replied. "Here, have some," he said, taking hold of a bunch of them for her. "I've got an old potato bag in the shed you can put them in."

"Thank you very much," she said. "You're a gem," which were the exact words she used to say to his dad when he'd freely give her some of his vegetables.

She sniffed the parsnips which she always loved immediately after they'd been dug up. They brought back memories of when she was a child, when her grandad used to bring some home from the farm. Geraldine's parents were from Ireland, where she used to go every summer for her holidays. They'd come over to Coventry in the 50s when the rebuilding was taking place after the war.

"I'm planting my garlic and shallots next week," she said. "You can get some from the main shed on Saturday if you want."

"I might just do that," he replied, not really knowing what he was going to do with his yearly harvest of vegetables.

Geraldine looked at him knowingly and said, "I always plant a lot more than I need and give some away to a local food bank, which always welcomes fresh vegetables."

"That's a good idea," agreed Jim, "I might do the same."

That evening Jim was going through some of the many books that his dad had about planting and growing vegetables and how there was a timetable or schedule for doing things. Jim's dad used to say that all these books will be useless in the future because of climate change. And Jim remembered him once furious, stomping around the house, angry that there was frost in the middle of June which killed the heads of his potatoes that had sprouted.

One of the books talked about the importance of top dressing the fruit trees and soft fruit bushes with a general fertiliser at this time of year to give them a boost. This made sense to Jim, so the next day he went to the garden centre, got some fertiliser and spread it around the fruit trees and bushes at the allotment. He also gave them a good pruning because they hadn't been picked as much since his mum passed away.

His mum had looked after the fruit trees and bushes, Jim now remembered. The jam she used to make was delicious and as a child he would go on errands for her dropping jars of jam round to elderly neighbours. The smell of stewed apple in the saucepan and apple pies in the oven came back to him while he was attending to the fruit trees. But also the awful stink of the horse manure that his dad used to get from the farm to put down on the soil.

Jim smiled when he thought back over such memories. His dad hadn't force him to come along to the allotment - he just accepted that his son wanted to do other things, probably like him when he was a child. Jim didn't have any children, but he thought how difficult it must be when you're passionate about something and want to pass it on to your children, only for them to go in another direction.

At the weekend Jim went to the main shed and bought some garlic cloves, onion bulbs and shallots for planting as Geraldine had recommended. He also got a few bags of early potatoes which he put in his shed ready for chitting. Jim was going through the exact routine that his dad used to as he knew no other way. He was even putting linseed oil on the wooden handles of the shed tools and checking that the watering can and buckets didn't leak, and the wheelbarrow didn't have a flat tyre.

Jim enjoyed the planting process. He lined everything up methodically via a string tied to two pegs either side of the plot. The soil was soft and well fertilised from the compost he had put down. Jim looked at the two large, open places where his dad used to make compost from unwanted vegetables and lawn cuttings. He'd bring eggs shells down from the house, saying they were good for compost.

Jim was quite happy when he had finished, looking at the seeds and bulbs sowed neatly into the soil. It was like they had been placed in a new home, he thought, as he watered them gently. He also sowed some lettuce seeds and other vegetables in trays for the greenhouse.

Jim felt content walking along the pathway of the allotment setting off home as the birds sang from the trees. He had not talked to anyone the whole time he was there today but had found solace in doing simple, but necessary things. The allotment is like an oasis in the middle of a city, he thought, away from everything that is going on in the world.

Chapter 4 – Something's Got to Change

There was a sense of urgency at the Extinction Rebellion meeting the following week. Coronavirus was spreading rapidly across Europe and it looked like the UK was heading for a lockdown. "Why haven't we closed our borders," people were asking, "like New Zealand and Australia? It's very simple." They were also saying that the Prime Minister had his head in the clouds after his December election victory while the Government should have been concentrating on this coming pandemic which was now very imminent.

"It's crazy," Geraldine said, "and inhumane how they're taking people with the virus out of hospitals and putting them into care homes. It's going to spread like wildfire and a lot of people are going to die."

"Yes, just like the fire in the Amazon rainforest at the start of the year," someone else said.

"It's the fact that we're out of balance that all this is happening," another person joined in. "We've had SARs, Ebola and now this. The planet is trying to tell us something."

"Yes," replied Geraldine, "and the volcanic ash from Iceland about ten years ago which put a stop to flights. Do you remember that?"

"Scientists have been telling us for years that we need to change what we're doing."

"What will happen if we don't?" asked someone holding a drink with a trembling hand.

"We could all be wiped out," said Geraldine, "and sooner than we think."

While this serious discussion was going on, Jim couldn't stop thinking about his dad and how he was always saying that something big had to happen for climate change to be put at the top of the agenda.

At the end of the meeting everyone made sure that they'd exchanged mobile numbers and had each other's email address as they weren't too sure when they would be meeting up again. Geraldine had heard from another group that they were planning to go on Zoom for their meetings, so this was something she was going to look into. It was all very strange and eerie as they left and said goodbye that evening and headed home.

"The roads are very quiet," Jim said, as Geraldine pulled up outside his house.

"People are scared out of their skin," said Geraldine. "It's crazy how people can suddenly become so fearful."

Jim wanted to cheer her up as she was usually so positive and determined about what she was doing.

"I'll see you at the allotment tomorrow then?" he said, getting out of the car.

"You will. At least there will be some normality there."

~ ~ ~

There were a lot of people at the allotment the following morning. Jim thought that they must be making the most of this lockdown period, especially those on furlough. The older guys will have to come even earlier, he thought, if they want to get the peace and tranquillity they usually found.

What Jim noticed was that everyone was talking - even people who were normally quiet and kept to themselves. He heard snippets of their conversations while watering. They were talking about the Cheltenham horse racing festival which had remained on the other week and which attracted so many people.

"They'll go back home now and take the virus with them," Jim heard someone say.

"What about that European football match the other evening at Anfield? The same will happen. It was a Spanish team. Liverpool played and thousands of fans came over. Part of Spain was already in lockdown and, still, 3000 fans entered the country. It's crazy."

"The Government hasn't a clue how to manage things."

"What about all the toilet rolls that people are hoarding from the supermarkets."

"It's ridiculous."

Jim was thinking that all he had heard was true. It appeared the virus had just come out of nowhere, but it hadn't. The leaders of the country knew it was coming and just hadn't prepared. Jim walked down to the tap to fill his watering can up again and felt angry inside. Had they been to Scouts and Guides as youngsters and forgotten the motto?

"They just don't listen to the scientists," was what his dad used to rant. And he was right.

"What's wrong with you, Jim?" asked Geraldine, back to her chirpy self, as she came up behind him at the tap as the water overflowed from the top of his can.

Jim got a start and turned off the tap.

"I'm alright, thanks. It's just…I've been listening to what people are talking about and can't believe what is happening. The world's gone mad."

"It's been mad for quite a while," replied Geraldine. "Just not many noticed. Most people were too concerned with their own lives. Come on, let's go for a walk over in the park by the river to the new meadow."

Jim laid down his watering can and followed Geraldine and Theo. He felt the fresh air as he went through the gate into the park and saw the mass of green. It still enveloped him like it did when he was a child racing down the hill. He could think of nothing else for a few seconds as he walked slowly behind Geraldine towards the river.

Geraldine turned around and said to him, "You like it here, don't you?"

"I do," replied Jim. "It reminds me of when I came here as a youngster with my football under my arm."

Geraldine smiled, but said nothing. They headed towards the meadow that had all sorts of wild flowers growing around the edge of the pond which was part of the new nature attraction.

"I sometimes get migraines," said Geraldine, "and a walk around here always does me good, even if it doesn't stop them completely. I love the scent of the flowers and the different birds they attract."

"It's a great addition to the park, especially as spring has arrived."

"Now, what was bothering you back there?" asked Geraldine.

"It's just what people are saying about the Coronavirus and how the Government should have acted sooner. They should have listened to the scientists and been prepared. It's going to cost us a lot of lives."

"Let me tell you a story about many people who join our Extinction Rebellion group. They first come full of enthusiasm and want to change things. Then they go into a sombre mood when they discover everything that is happening to the planet and that time is running out. It's called mourning - thinking of future generations and how difficult life will be for them. Scientists have been telling governments about the situation for years and not much has happened. In fact, it's getting worse."

"It's hard to accept," said Jim.

"It is," Geraldine replied, "and it's the same with the Coronavirus. The Government knew about it long before we did but didn't act."

"What are we going to do?" asked Jim.

"I don't know, Jim, but for the moment we're going to go back to our vegetable plots as we both have a lot of work to do there."

"Yes, we do," Jim laughed, as they walked back alongside the gentle, flowing river towards the allotments.

Summer

Chapter 5 - The Drought

Before Jim moved down to London in the early 90s, he was into raves and drugs in quite a serious way. He worked during the week for a local accountancy firm, but at weekends he would be out partying in the evenings until the early hours. He was a regular at The Eclipse in Coventry, one of the first all-night clubs in the country. He made friends there and would also go around the country raving, sometimes to The Hacienda in Manchester. He liked the buzz of drugs and was finding it harder and harder returning to normality on Monday mornings. He was on a low in the week compared to the high he experienced at weekends. It was such a contrast; he was like two different characters. In the week he wouldn't say much to anyone, just keep quiet, doing what was expected of him. But on the weekends, while drugged up, he would come out of himself and be talking to everyone.

Jim also liked football from an early age and used to play in the Sunday league. He had been pretty good on the wing. His mum and dad weren't into football, but they still encouraged him and went along to see him play. He lost interest in his late teens, but still followed and supported his local club.

Some of the guys that Jim met on Saturday afternoons at the match also went to raves at The Eclipse and so the circle of people that he knew was growing. They used to enjoy trouble with opposing fans at the matches and Jim liked being part of something bigger than himself. It was the adrenaline that it created and the risk of being arrested. It was all part of his high at the weekends.

Jim was getting a bit of a name for himself as he was just over six feet tall and quite well built. This helped in the drug circles and he would always stay calm regardless of what was happening. He attracted people as he could be quiet and sombre, but would always have a good laugh too. He was also able to read people and situations very well.

Jim always felt though, regardless of how good a time he was having, that there was something missing in his life. He had had many girlfriends, but nothing really lasted long. He could never put his finger on why that was. It was as if he needed something but didn't know what it was or where to find it. He sometimes felt like he was just going through the motions, both at work and at weekends.

Jim's move to London was fortunate for him. He'd almost been arrested at football matches for causing trouble with the away fans a few times. He was also getting into dealing drugs and was convinced that he was being watched and followed by the CID.

The job opportunity came out of nowhere. Jim wasn't looking to enhance his career, but a job came up at a growing accountancy firm linked to the one where he was currently working. His boss told him that he should apply for it, so he phoned up, enquired, filled out an application form and sent it off, and then thought nothing more of it. Two weeks later he went down to London for an interview, got offered the job, and planned to move. It all happened so quickly!

It was what Jim needed. The accountancy firm was just taking off and required somebody with his knowledge. They were young people working there and he got on well with them. They liked going out for a drink after work on Fridays but weren't into drugs, however, Jim didn't seem to need drugs as much these days. He had the odd spliff in the evenings, but nothing like he was using back home.

At first, he came home every other weekend to see his parents and watch his team play football. He went out a few times in the evenings, but was conscious not to overdo it as he would be thinking about his week ahead at work. He was ultimately becoming more responsible and growing up. But he still had that nagging feeling of wanting to do something different with his life, something that mattered.

Jim progressed well with his career in London and after two years got a more lucrative job in the city, working on pensions. He liked how everyone was excited about taking risks and making money over a short period of time and then investing it in another commodity or asset class. In a weird sort of way, it gave him a similar adrenalin kick that he used to get at football matches with opposing fans or going to an illegal acid-house rave. It was living on the edge and Jim's calm composure always helped him to work out problems which meant everyone liked him.

It was strange how Jim ended up working in finance. His parents were not money orientated and didn't raise him to focus on money and expensive presents. In fact, they bought him books more than anything else and Jim didn't mind as he devoured them. His dad was a Star Trek fan which appealed to Jim and they would sit down and watch it together. They were also admirers of Star Wars and queued up for ages at the cinema to watch the films when they were first released; his dad always the most excited.

Although Jim made a lot of money working in London, it still wasn't what he desired the most. That was something else, but he didn't know what and was maybe one of the reasons why he was popular at work and why he did so well. There was a mysticism about him that no one could fathom, including himself. He was like someone constantly digging, but at the same time didn't know what he was digging for.

~ ~ ~

Jim thought that he was watering the plot of his allotment much more than he did when he used to help his dad. Then he laughed to himself as he remembered how his dad used to be so pleased with the April showers raining down on his sown seeds prompting green shoots.

"Look at them shooting up. My rain dance has worked," he would shout, as they tilted and bent after the shower had stopped. "They just love a bit of gentle rain."

There aren't many April showers this year, thought Jim, as he stomped to the tap again to refill his watering can. He was thinking that the charges would surely go up soon because of the amount of water they were all using.

It wasn't always like this, he thought. Maybe in July or August, but never in April and May.

"Hi Jim," said Geraldine, as she appeared by his gate with Theo beside her, wagging his tail. "I see you're doing a lot of watering."

"Yes, I've never known it to be this dry so early in the year. Nothing will grow if it's not watered."

"This is how it's going to be with climate change. I tend to sow things that need less watering like peas and beans."

"What's it going to be like in the future?"

"God only knows, unless there's some drastic action taken."

"It's been so hot for this time of year and the soil is rock hard. The seedlings don't know what's going on."

"I don't want to sound pessimistic, but it's going to get worse if we don't reduce carbon emissions and the temperature keeps rising. In places like Madagascar it's a lot worse with the drought and famine they're having."

"My dad used to go on about all the CO2 emissions coming from fossil fuels."

"Almost 90%. And what's worse is this industry is subsidised by governments. It's as if they're trying to destroy us."

"It's the bigger picture we should be looking at and not just the current virus. It's the climate emergency that is the real pandemic."

"Exactly."

Chapter 6 – New Beginnings

After Jim said goodbye to Geraldine, he packed away his tools in the shed. He was feeling depressed again by everything that was happening; the coronavirus, the lockdown, climate change. It felt that not only his life (with him losing his dad and returning home with no job or idea about what he was going to do), but the whole world had been brought to a standstill. The roads were quiet, with no rush hour traffic, as most people - apart from essential workers - were at home. It felt eerie in the mornings as Jim went down to the allotment. And to make matters worse, he badly needed a haircut, but all the barbers and hairdressers were closed.

Geraldine had said, just before she departed, that maybe the lockdown will give everyone a reality check on how things will be if we don't make the necessary changes to our lives and how it will give us the opportunity to reset ourselves. Jim pondered this as he took the long way back home, next to the running river and by the meadow. It lifted his spirits as he was able to forget about everything, if only for a short time, assimilating the scent of the wildflowers and listening to the stream flowing gently.

He still thought that he needed to do something. He had that nagging feeling in the pit of his stomach that had started in his late teens going to raves and getting into trouble at football matches and which had never really gone away. He'd tried different things to find his true purpose in life, but had never found it.

Jim walked close to the river and stood watching the stream flow by effortlessly. How does it do it so easily? he thought. It simply goes around any obstacles it faces. Watching the stream brought back memories from his childhood when he used to run in the park with his football. Those sunny days when everyone was smiling and having a good time seemed far away in the distant past now.

He kept listening to the clear stream that was the River Sherbourne as it had a kind of extra resonance today. He thought back to earlier times, maybe to a previous life, when this river must have been vital for early settlers and a useful resource during the medieval period. It would have been essential as everyone needed it.

The stream stayed in Jim's head for a while after he left the park. It seemed to soothe him and tell him that everything would be alright. Its sound had a special ringing to it and Jim thought of the adversities that people had come through over the ages.

When Jim got back to the house, he started to tidy up the place. The house needed a lot of work because his dad had been so busy with environmental issues that he hadn't much time for DIY. Jim had planned to take down the old wallpaper and give the place a fresh new coat of paint and maybe get new carpets and curtains in. He thought through such plans when packing up his things in London.

Now, however, he felt something pressing that needed to be done. There seemed to be an urgency in the air, as if he had been waiting for this moment for a long time - in fact, all his life.

Jim cleared the old table in the living room and sat down with a cup of tea which he placed on a coaster beside him. He looked down at the table and wondered how old it was and how many things and people it must have seen over the years. It was an antique and had previously belonged to his dad's parents who'd lived in Scotland. He could see the lines of the wood and how they curved around the little circles. They reminded him of the lines on his parents' faces as they grew older with age and experience, perhaps needed in order to pass on their wisdom.

Jim looked up from the table at the shelf in front of him, full of books and magazines. His eyes were drawn to a pad of A4 paper half hanging out between them. He got up, extracted it, then took a pen from the drawer, sat down again and began to write.

He wasn't too sure what he was writing at first, but after a while he became aware that it might be a poem of some sort. He wasn't thinking about what he was writing, just letting his subconscious pour onto the page. He felt free, freer than he'd ever felt. It was as if he had suddenly found the escape route which he had been searching for and a valve had been released. He forgot about everything else as he started writing.

Jim had no idea what time it was when he eventually looked up from the pad of paper now full of words, but he noticed it was slowly getting dark outside. He hadn't thought about eating or anything when writing; it was as if he had travelled into another universe. He put down his pen on the old table, next to the cup of tea that had long gone cold and went into the kitchen to prepare dinner.

He was very content that evening, putting his feet up on the pouffe, reading his book as usual, and not worrying about things as he usually did.

Jim woke up earlier than normal the next morning, quickly showered, had breakfast, and then sat down at the table to begin writing again. He continued this process every morning and it became part of his day. He could hear the birds tweeting outside, busy making nests and he felt he was now busy too with his writing.

Jim didn't have a clear direction with his writing, but knew it was mostly to do with change and how everything is going to be different. He felt it should matter to everyone - the rich, the poor and the homeless, because it's going to affect all our lives. The words kept flowing, as if there was a message that needed to get out.

Jim's eccentric English teacher at school had encouraged him upon Jim writing a poem in class. The teacher had typed it up and given it back to Jim and said that it was very good work. Jim didn't think much of it as a teenager and didn't explore poetry further. But he never forgot his teacher being so pleased when giving him his poem back.

After spending the mornings writing, Jim would go to his allotment in the afternoons, walk around the plot, do some weeding, watering or whatever was needed. The seedlings are slow, he thought, but beginning to make progress.

"You have an extra spring in your step today," said Geraldine, as she leant over the gate to Jim's plot.

"I've started writing in the mornings, even weekends, mainly doing some poems. Haven't looked at poetry since I was at school, but I like writing them. I can see the images more clearly when written down. Not sure what they're like, but they're doing me good."

"I can see that," said Geraldine, looking at his face and noticing how there was a sparkle in his eyes that wasn't there before. "You must show them to me some time...when you're ready."

"OK. You can be the first person to read over my work - be a critic, if you like."

"I would love that."

"Thank you, Geraldine."

"You'll be able to channel your energies into your writing. I use art and painting to channel mine. You must join the Positive Images poetry workshop. They used to meet in the library before the lockdown, but I think they still meet online. I'll find out and let you know."

"That would be great. Thanks."

Jim wiped his brow with his shirt, which was drenched with sweat and said, "Isn't it hot today. I've never known May to be this hot before."

"I was reading that it's been one of the hottest since records began in 1880."

"I remember '76 was very warm, but I don't think it was this early in the year."

"Summers are going to get hotter as temperatures rise. That reminds me, we're resuming our Extinction Rebellion meetings on Zoom if you'd like to join us again - that is if you can spare some time from your writing."

"Yes, I would," said Jim. "Let us know when they are and send me the links."

Geraldine quietly smiled at Jim, before saying goodbye and walking off through the gate, into the park and towards the meadow.

Jim seemed like a reformed person with a new perspective. Everything started to appear different to him and have fresh meaning. It wasn't a chore spending the mornings writing; it was as if he'd been given a present that he would never tire of. He carried a little notebook around with him for the rest of the day and would scribble words down if something caught his attention - even mundane things like two pigeons being noisy in his garden over scraps of bread he'd left out. Everything seemed to matter to him much more now he was writing.

As Geraldine had said, writing was a release for him. All the pent-up frustration over the years with no real direction in life was coming out of him. He was crafting his work as well, deliberating over it, leaving it and then going back to it. It was like he was shining an ornament and wanted to make it as bright as he possibly could.

The lockdown restrictions began to ease, and pubs were opening up again. Jim felt there was a great sense of comfort among people and not the usual rush and need to do things as there often was during the summer. It was as if everyone was coming out of an extended hibernation. People seemed to have more time to talk to each other and were concerned for their neighbours - especially elderly people living alone. Jim wasn't really up for clapping the NHS staff on Thursday evenings, as he felt they should be better paid instead, but he often went out and chatted to the neighbours, most of whom were new to the area and weren't around when Jim first lived here. There were families, young children playing together, and people talking more than ever, avoiding isolation.

This relaxing mood in people seemed to help with Jim's writing too. He was compiling an anthology of poems, diligently working on it and developing it. He was now part of the Positive Images poetry workshop which included people of all ages, cultures and backgrounds. A whole new world was opening up for Jim as he was finding his own, unique voice and style and learning from other writers too.

Jim started going to The Plough again for a drink or two. He missed being with his dad though, as they used to enjoy going together, especially during his last six months when Jim returned. Jim, by way of solace, would get out his notepad and start writing, normally constructing a poem – something new or half finished. His writing was like a new friend whom he could rely on at any time. He would block out all the noise and everyone around him as if sat there by himself with a pint, notepad and pen, concentrating solely on what he was doing.

Geraldine would sometimes join him for lunch at The Plough on Sunday afternoons. Jim could talk very freely with Geraldine and showed her some of his poems, which she would read, take away and then later give her opinion on. She was a good critic, not simply saying if they were admirable or poor, but giving him an honest appraisal. Geraldine knew that Jim was just venturing out, seeking a truth in his writing like many artists, and that such a path was long and arduous. Many do it for a while but then get distracted by events or things that happen in their lives. Geraldine didn't think that Jim was one of those people.

Jim's allotment was coming on well and he was beginning to harvest some of the early vegetables that he had sown from the greenhouse. The strawberries that his mum had planted many years ago, and he had cut back in the early spring, were producing so much fruit this year. Jim had to give a lot of them away to other members of the allotment and to his neighbours, whom he had gotten to know from Thursday evenings. They were delicious and much nicer than the ones Jim bought from the supermarket.

The onions and green vegetables were also very tasty. Jim liked the process of going out to the allotment, digging up the vegetables, bringing them back and cooking them. It was simple, but therapeutic. There was no driving needed and Jim often thought that this is exactly what his forefathers did.

Jim also liked going to the allotment in the evenings as the days were longer at the height of summer. Everything seemed more relaxed at this time. Some people would be out watering their vegetables, but not doing too much. It was as if they were winding down after a long day. Jim would sometimes get the old chair out of the shed and sit down and take it all in; the birds singing, the leaves on the trees gently rustling in the light breeze, the flower buds at the side of the plot giving off a scent, and bees making a little noise finishing off their day's work gathering pollen. This is magic, he thought, and just wanted to grasp the moment and hold on to it.

He then laughed to himself as he thought of his dad sitting in this chair, getting out his pipe, filling it with tobacco and lighting it. There was that whirl and smell of tobacco smoke that used to come from him as Jim was playing around the allotment as a child. But his dad just sat there, very still and content, with his pipe in his mouth, taking in the moment and probably thinking the same as Jim right now.

The next day, after Jim had finished his morning writing, he went to B&Q to get some paint as he'd decided to paint his shed at the allotment. He'd fixed a few things like the leak in the guttering, but thought the shed could do with some further attention. He went for a bright colour, similar to the football club that he used to follow.

It was a hot day and Jim took his top off while painting the shed. He was getting a good tan from being outside most days and looking healthy - much more so than when he was working ridiculous hours in London. He was also regaining strength in his limbs from the digging and weeding he was doing, and thought this the best type of exercise he had ever done.

Jim stood back, observing his work after he had finished. The shed looked good in its new sky blue colour and Jim liked it immensely. He would definitely be able to spot it as soon as he came through the main gate.

"That's a handy bit of work," said Geraldine, smiling as she leant over the fence to his plot, with Theo wagging his tail beside her.

"Thank you," said Jim.

"You might want to do mine while you're at it," said Geraldine, "although I think I'll go for a darker colour."

Jim laughed and said "OK, no problem."

~ ~ ~

It was the summer solstice the following day and Jim remembered coming here for it with his parents when he was small. They wouldn't do much work on the allotment - just bring a picnic and a blanket to sit on, and often stroll down the hill, holding hands, while Jim ran ahead of them.

It's funny, Jim thought, how he could vividly remember those days even though he was a young child at the time.

"I was down here for sunrise this morning," said Geraldine. "It was magnificent - best it's been for a few years."

"Wow - that must have been great. I'll come down next year. My parents used to celebrate the solstice."

"I know. I used to see them down here when you were in London. There'd be a few of us and we'd go over to the small hill in the park to get a good view. Your parents were special people - very connected."

"I didn't know that they still came here to watch the sun rise during the summer solstice while I was in London."

Geraldine just smiled at him, as they sat down together on the grass.

"In fact, I think there are a lot of things I don't know about my parents."

"It's the same with us all," said Geraldine. "Our parents know each other a long time before we're born, so there're many things we don't know. But the main thing to remember is that our parents loved us, and I know that yours truly loved you."

This struck a deep chord with Jim and he couldn't say anything as a lump appeared in his throat. He just put out his hand and took hold of the hand of Geraldine, who didn't resist. They sat like this for some time, not saying anything, just looking out as the small breeze caught the leaves in the trees above Jim's vegetable plot. Listening to the birds and feeling the texture and warmth of each other's hand, they seemed content.

"We've got another meeting this evening if you're free," said Geraldine, after what appeared to be a very long time.

"Yes, I made a note on my phone and it reminded me earlier."

"Great. We'll be discussing our involvement in the demos in London at the beginning of September."

"I've been reading up on the internet about the demos from last year."

"Yes, there were loads of us there and we made some noise on the streets. OK, I'll see you later then."

"Yes, see you later."

Chapter 8 – Summer Holidays

Jim's parents lived in a double bay terraced house in an area known as Poets Corner which had roads named after famous poets. Jim's grandmother, who had lived on the Isle of Arran, liked the fact that her son and family lived in Poets Corner as she was very fond of poetry and would always be telling Jim, when they came to visit, that he would be a great poet one day.

Jim was a very quiet boy growing up as an only child, with his head always in a book. And it was the same when they used to go up on the train to Scotland to visit his grandparents. They would all be reading, and Jim felt grown up, like he was on the same level. His parents would talk to him as if he was an adult and always ask what he thought or what his view was. Jim didn't say much, but liked it, as he never heard his friends' parents asking them for their opinions.

The train journey up to Glasgow would be enjoyable for the three of them. Jim's mum would prepare lots of sandwiches and would let Jim have one whenever he liked. Jim would stop reading his book after a while to look out of the window at the green fields whizzing past.

Being brought up in a city he never saw much of this apart from when they went out for a drive in the country. It felt to Jim, from a very early age, like he was going back to the place he belonged when travelling up to Scotland. He couldn't quite put his finger on what it was that appealed to him most about his dad's birth place. Was it that it was on an island, surrounded by the sea and cut off from the rest of the country? Was it the quality of the air, the green fields and the people he met who he seemed to find a deep connection with? He just liked the place so much and couldn't understand why anybody would want to leave it.

On the train journey up to Glasgow, his dad would worry about his allotment. His neighbour was going to water the vegetables if they went through a dry patch, but nobody would give them the care and attention that Jim's dad did.

"And what if the allotment gets vandalised while I'm away? What will we do then?"

Jim's mum would say nothing, but smile to herself thinking that he cares so much about his vegetables.

Jim used to read up and find out all he could about the places that the train would stop at including Preston, Lancaster and Carlisle. He was like a magnet for knowledge, discovering new locations that he'd never been to, apart from briefly stopping at their station platforms. His mum and dad would ask him what he knew about the place where the train pulled in and he'd rather reluctantly reveal information that astounded them.

From Glasgow they would get a connection to Ardrossan and head west for the coast. There would be no more reading at this point for the three of them and not much talking either – instead, they'd simply be taking it all in, eyes fixed through the window, as if they were going back in time looking at a landscape that was no more.

The ferry crossing from Ardrossan to Brodick was the best part of the journey for Jim. They were almost at the island, but Jim savoured every part of it - the fresh air, the smell of the sea salt, the waves splashing up on the ferry. It all felt so real, so true, like he was returning to his long-lost homeland.

As the ferry approached the harbour, they could see Jim's dad's parents waiting patiently for them. They were so pleased to see them and once they'd arrived the two would run towards Jim and wrap their arms around him. He was their only grandchild.

The journey back to their house in their old Ford Cortina didn't take long. Jim's grandmother would always cook them a good roast dinner with plenty of vegetables from their garden and they would talk all evening and include Jim in their conversations. He strangely didn't miss having someone around his own age.

Jim liked spending time with his dad and grandad, and they would go fishing some days. They would also do some work in the garden which had a large area for growing vegetables at the back of the house with an orchard as well. Jim's grandparents were keen on growing their own and being self-sufficient. The soil was of good quality on the island and the vegetables grew very well. Jim used to like digging with a small spade that his grandad made for him, on the neat beds they had and he used to wipe sweat off his brow as he had seen his dad and grandad do.

There was an old plough in the orchard near the shed belonging to Jim's great grandad, who had also lived and worked on the island. Jim was fascinated with it and would spend hours as a child sitting beside it asking what it did and how it worked. "That plough goes back generations," Jim's grandad would say, resting his hand on it admiringly. "It's ploughed many fields, this one has."

They also picked berries to take home and make delicious pies and jams from. They had strawberries, blackberries, raspberries, gooseberries and other wild berries, which seemed to taste so much nicer on the island. Jim's grandmother loved cooking and being in the kitchen making things, not only for her family, but for many of her neighbours as well.

They enjoyed coastal walks on the island, especially in the morning before breakfast. The fresh air felt so clean to Jim and it would give rise to good appetites before they came back and had a cooked breakfast. Jim's grandparents would devote all their time to them when they came to visit, which was normally every summer. They came down to visit them in England too, but this became less frequent as they grew older and didn't like travelling so much. They were content with their simple life on the island though.

In the evenings after dinner, they would sit around the log fire in the main living room of the house and Jim's grandparents would get their musical instruments out and start playing traditional Scottish tunes, and sing songs. His grandmother played the fiddle and his grandad the piano accordion. Jim's dad would also sing the odd song that he'd learnt as a child and they would all join in. His grandad would tell stories too from long ago, and his grandmother would recite a few poems.

Such evenings also appealed to Jim's mum, who was brought up on the mainland of Scotland, near Glasgow. She had a good voice and could sing some traditional Scottish folk songs like 'The Bonnie Banks of Loch Lomond'. Jim, meanwhile, would sit with them, very content, soaking it all in and quietly tapping his foot to the rhythm of the music.

Jim's mum became very attached to her in-laws and kept in regular contact with them upon returning to England. Both of her parents had passed away at an early age, before Jim was born. It was how she got into needlework and knitting as these were great passions of Jim's grandmother. They would swap patterns and knit similar items of clothing that were passed to a charity for orphaned children they both became involved with.

Saying goodbye to Jim's grandparents at Brodick Port in order to return to the mainland was the hardest part of their visit. Tears would be streaming down Jim's grandmother's face as she hugged them all tightly, while his grandad stood very still, puffing smoke from his pipe and gripping hold of his cap with both hands.

"It's not as if we're emigrating to America," Jim's dad would say, trying to put on a brave face.

"I know," she would reply, "but it will be a long time 'til we see you three again. Do keep in touch now, won't you all."

"We will - of course," Jim's mum would say, "and you can send me a copy of your new pattern when it arrives."

"I will indeed, love," she would say, as she wiped another tear off her cheek as Jim and his parents gave a final wave, turned around and walked slowly onto the boat.

Autumn

Chapter 9 - The Demo

Jim always liked the end of August and beginning of September with the leaves on the trees turning red, later becoming a golden colour. He noticed the balance of things - summer had not yet ended and autumn hadn't quite begun. There was a centrality about this time of year that made Jim feel rooted and riveted to his very being.

"Are you ready for tomorrow?" asked Geraldine, as they met on the pathway returning from the allotment after doing some more work on their plots.

"Yes, I'm ready. Looking forward to it too. Be my first time down in London since I moved everything back up here."

"That's good. Meet you at eight at the station then?"

"Yes, I'll be there."

"Some other people said they're coming too."

"That's great - the more the better."

Jim was going with Geraldine to London to meet up with other Extinction Rebellion groups from around the country and actively take part in demonstrations at prominent places to highlight the need for action on climate change. They were catching an early train and intended to take part in the march to Parliament Square, and then listen to the many speakers plus get encouragement from other activists.

Jim couldn't believe he was going on a climate change demo as he'd never imagined being involved in this kind of protest. But he did remember his dad phoning him once, all excited about the Paris Agreement in 2015. He also remembered the demonstrations in London a couple years ago. He had just walked out on his job in the city and wasn't taking much notice, but became aware of groups of people occupying major bridges and the disruptions that ensued.

Geraldine was talking to two of their local group members who were also travelling down on the train to London. Extinction Rebellion's third demand of 'Decide Together' was being discussed; in other words, ordinary people forming a Citizens' Assembly like they had in France, Belgium, Poland and Ireland. Jim, meanwhile, was looking out of the window and reflecting on how much his life had changed over the last two years since moving back home - his dad dying, working on the allotment, starting to write poetry and getting involved in activism. He was a completely different person.

They had had a meeting online last night to make sure they were all OK about taking part in the demonstration. They were part of an Affinity Group, had specific roles, and knew what each other were doing. It helped reassure some of the members - concerned that they might get arrested at the protest, as they had children or jobs they didn't want to lose - to hear that only a small number of people tended to get arrested from the vast pool present, and that there were support mechanisms firmly in place. People of all ages were going to be there.

Jim looked out of the window again and thought back to the days when he was a football hooligan, meeting up with his mates in town and going to a match intent on looking for trouble. It was the comradeship he enjoyed most of all, being with others and knowing that someone would be watching his back. But this was different. He was not going for the excitement, but to be surrounded by people who wanted to change things.

Geraldine had been to many demonstrations in the past and asked Jim if he'd been to any, noticing how calm and collected he was as he walked the streets of London with the others, not far behind a Samba band. It was like Jim had participated for years. He was very relaxed as he walked with people of the same mindset; wanting the Government to act. He talked to many of them, from different backgrounds and professions - including several doctors and GPs - who had travelled from all over the country to take part in the demonstration. They reached Parliament Square where they listened to several speakers talking about the urgency of the climate situation and how drastic change was needed. Many were saying that the Covid pandemic was only a small wave in comparison to the climate breakdown we were heading for.

Coming back on the train, the Midlands group were tired after the day's march in London, plus listening to the speakers. Geraldine's voice was hoarse as well from all the chanting that she'd done. They were encouraged though by the size of the gathering and assortment of people they had seen - committed individuals from all walks of life. Jim could see that these people were not just going to return to work on Monday morning and continue with their normal lives. He knew by their determination that they were going to fight on until changes were made.

Chapter 10 – The Harvest

At the allotment Jim was enjoying harvesting the vegetables. The leeks, after a slow start, had grown well and he had to be careful when pulling them from the soil. He'd also dug up the onions and left them to dry, and put the potatoes into large paper sacks that he'd found to store them.

"You might need another plot next year the way you're going, Jim," Geraldine said, as she and Theo walked past his plot one afternoon. "I can put your name on the waiting list if you like," she laughed.

"You'd better not," laughed Jim.

"What I sometimes do with the beans is blanch them first and then put them in the freezer. That way they keep their goodness and you can just have them whenever you want."

"That's a good idea. I'll try that."

Jim liked the root vegetables and would often roast them in the oven. He would sprinkle fresh herbs on them that he'd also grown and leave the vegetables cooking which created an aroma around the house that reminded him of relaxing Sunday afternoons he'd had as a boy. His dad would have his feet up on the pouffe reading a newspaper or book and his mum would be in the kitchen cooking dinner listening to music.

Jim missed his parents so much. He seemed to miss his mum more now that his dad was gone too. It was just the simple, ordinary things they used to do that meant so much. Those letters his mum would write to him every week while he worked down in London, filling him in on what was going on in their neighbourhood. Or his dad phoning him every Sunday, without fail, to talk with him about how his football team was doing.

Jim still liked going to the allotment at the end of the day, when he had finished his writing, and the birds were quietly singing close to dusk. He had to go earlier now that the days were getting shorter and there was a slight chill in the air. The seasons are changing, he thought, as he dug up some more vegetables to have in the evening. He thought back to when his dad told him how his family used to help the local farmer during harvest time, collecting potatoes from the dark, Scottish soil, putting them into sacks and storing them for the long winter ahead. It was an annual ritual where men, women and children would help. The locals would work hard together in the husbandry of the potatoes and when the work was done they would all enjoy a harvest supper.

Those were the days, Jim thought, that harvesting had to be done and stored away before the weather turned. If it wasn't, there wouldn't be enough food to get through the winter. It was crucially important and a necessity and that is why everyone helped.

Jim was thinking about this as he tipped the vegetables into the wheelbarrow and pushed it up to his shed, then sat down on an old stool he'd left outside. What would happen, he thought, if we couldn't grow vegetables anymore? He had read that there were already problems in the Global South with more intense droughts and floods causing crop failure. And it was even happening here with the cost of certain foods going up due to poor harvests. He'd seen a documentary on the internet about soil and how it was deteriorating from the use of chemicals and pesticides. One specialist said that in 60 years' time we won't be able to grow anything as the soil is losing its biodiversity. What will happen then? Jim shuddered to think.

Jim carefully placed the vegetables he'd dug up into his rucksack, put the wheelbarrow back in the shed, closed the door and locked up. He put his bag over his shoulder and walked up the path to the gate of the allotment. He was feeling despondent, but not as much as before attending the demo in London. Knowing that there were so many other people thinking the same as him helped. And not only were they thinking about the planet, they were doing something about it.

"How are things, Jim?" Geraldine asked, as she walked up beside him once he was through the gate.

"Better for having seen you," said Jim. "You always seem to pop up at just the right time."

Geraldine smiled and said, "We had a great time in London the other week, didn't we."

"We sure did," replied Jim, "and hopefully we've raised the issue more with people and the powers that be."

"That's what we're aiming to do. It's said that if we can cross the threshold of 3.5% of the population, then we'll be able to bring about change. It's what other movements worked towards like the Suffragettes and the Civil Rights Movement in America. We're getting there, but there's still lots to do."

"Wasn't I reading that a few celebrities are backing Extinction Rebellion?"

"Yes, there have been some such as actress Emma Thompson, singer Ellie Goulding and novelist Philip Pullman."

"We just need someone to keep pressing for action."

"You mean someone who can keep speaking up about how drastic action is needed?"

"What the planet needs is balance. If you keep taking away from something there'll be nothing left in the end. It's common sense."

"I know. It's like with our allotments. We replenish the soil each year with compost or manure and do crop rotation so all the goodness is not taken out of it. If we just kept planting the same seeds in the same place year after year without putting anything back into the soil, there wouldn't be much of a harvest after long. The Earth needs feeding, just like we do, and now is the time for our generation to reverse the system. It's why we're here. We can't be taking all of the time."

"It's just what I'm writing about in my poems," said Jim. "I think they're trying to tell me something, or giving me a message that we're approaching a very critical stage. We can just carry on with what we're doing and ignore all the signs around us, or we can act and do something about it."

"Many of the experts are calling it a tipping point. There'll be a stage where drastic change will be paramount - more important than anything else. After that there will be no turning back."

"It sounds quite drastic."

"It is - more than anything."

~ ~ ~

"The nature reserve is at its best in autumn," said Geraldine the next day, as they walked alongside the river in the park that flowed into the city centre.

"It sure is," replied Jim. "The scents it gives off are amazing. And there's going to be a harvest full moon tonight."

"I know," Geraldine said, as she gripped his hand tighter as they admired the many colours of the flowers which seemed so much brighter and alive now that they were together.

It had all happened quite naturally, as if they were meant to be together at this time and place. Jim and Geraldine were seeing each other at the allotment every day - sometimes twice when watering during the dry periods. Restrictions had eased and they'd go for Sunday lunches together at The Plough where Geraldine's Theo was also welcome.

Geraldine also called round at Jim's some evenings with vegetables from her allotment and would start preparing them for the two of them. Jim had shown her where the key was behind the house so she could let herself in if he was out.

It had simply been a platonic relationship; the two of them enjoying each other's company and learning from one another too. Until mid-summer's day, not long after the sale of Jim's flat in London had gone through, when Jim reached out and took hold of Geraldine's hand while they sat on the grass in the park. Since that moment there was a spark between them which they could both feel. They didn't say anything, but were aware of it every time they met.

So, one evening after they'd had dinner and were sitting on the settee as if they'd been together for years, Jim said quite casually, "Why don't you move in?"

And Geraldine replied, also quite casually, "OK then."

So that was it. The next day they booked a 'Man with a Van' to move Geraldine's things. She didn't have too much as she was living in a rented flat. Within 24 hours, Geraldine had moved her stuff into Jim's, and they were living together. It was all very straight forward.

It didn't change their lives drastically; Jim would still get up early, go to his study and cultivate his poetry, and in the afternoon head down to the allotment. Geraldine would not rise early, have a leisurely breakfast, and then work on campaigning for Extinction Rebellion - organising events and training material for new members as she was a rep for the Midlands area. Then, late afternoon, she would walk down to the allotments with Theo and meet Jim.

Everyone knew they were an item as they couldn't stop holding hands. It was like they had just planted a seed together, which needed careful attention and daily nurturing in order to grow.

Jim's perception and clarity in his writing had improved since Geraldine moved in. He could see things more clearly in his mind's eye - the colours, contrasts and nuances that many would miss, which improved his writing vastly. There began a kind of hunger in him to write - wanting to get it out of his system and onto the page. And in a strange way, the more he wrote, the more he wanted Geraldine.

Jim started reading some of the great Scottish literature that his grandmother had given to him many years ago, which was stored away in the loft. For some reason he always wanted to keep the books and got them down one day, marvelling at the novels, ballets and poems - their richness and relevance, even today. Jim's grandmother was particularly fond of Scotland's legendary poet, Robert Burns, known as The Ploughman Poet, being the son of a tenant's farmer. His poems, like 'To a Mouse', appealed to Jim and were read to him at a young age by his grandmother in her broad Scottish accent.

Jim kept writing, morning after morning, including weekends. It was like something new came to him each day with the sunrise; thoughts and ideas flowing out of him as if they'd been waiting to do this for years. It was as if a dam had suddenly burst open. Jim was in another world while writing, as if nothing else mattered. And he sometimes felt that his writing was in control of him, rather than the other way around. He would start off writing about one subject and would end on a completely different track.

He had decided to take part in the Positive Images poetry competition and so a poem of his needed to be submitted soon. Jim had been reading some of the poems from last year and found them to be of a very high quality - much better than his own, he thought - and therefore wondered if he had been writing for long enough and whether his entry was worthy. But Geraldine encouraged him, saying "It's the writing of poetry and the taking part that counts. And in November you'll all get together on Zoom to read out your poems. I went along last year when we weren't in lockdown and it was great hearing all the entrants, some better than others, but all spoken from the heart - sharing a bit of themselves...some for the first time."

This year's theme was Neighbourhoods and Jim had loads of ideas so was glad when Geraldine convinced him to take part. He was thinking of current neighbourhoods, neighbourhoods in the past and those in the future. He thought about how they'd changed over time and how they vary from place to place but should all have that common thread of community spirit running through them. After he'd finished his poem, he put it away for a while, to let it rest, and would come back to it in a few days.

As the weather was getting colder and the nights drawing in, Jim was spending less time at the allotment. There wasn't much he could do apart from harvest vegetables. They had two plots for one household, so were not buying vegetables at all. In fact, they had too much veg and so gave some away.

Jim decided to start working on the house in the afternoons, after writing in the morning - taking down wallpaper and painting one room at a time. Geraldine didn't mind as she often went over to her friend's to work. Jim quite enjoyed decorating and the smell of a newly-painted room gave off fresh, positive vibes.

Plus, he needed some physical exercise now he wasn't going to the allotment every day. And the painting of the house brought back many memories from his childhood - having friends round for parties and his parents always doing their best for him.

Geraldine helped Jim decide on the colours for the rooms. The things she wore, mostly from charity shops, looked so good on her which made Jim trust her judgement. She seemed to be able to bring the colours out of themselves. The garden was south facing, so they went for a light and neutral colour at the back of the house. At the front of the house, they went for a lavender hue which they both liked. Geraldine said it reminded her of the scent in her parents' garden when she was younger.

Geraldine started helping Jim with the painting after a while. Jim was grateful and was amazed how well she took to it and the dexterity that she had. She just absolutely knew what to do.

"We're going to finish this a lot quicker now that the two of us are doing it," said Jim.

"I don't think of it like that. I just try to enjoy what I'm doing and don't worry about time," replied Geraldine. "What is time anyway and does it matter if we finish tomorrow or next week? It is the doing that counts," she said, as she stroked the brush so effortlessly up and down the walls.

Jim couldn't answer that and just smiled at Geraldine as he dipped his brush in the paint tin again. Sometimes he wondered if Geraldine was the real poet as she held so much wisdom in her - just the simple things, like not being rushed by the crowd. He thought, as he continued painting, that perhaps he was writing in order to discover this unique simplicity - something that had always been there, but which he'd lost as he'd grown up.

Jim still felt that mornings were the best time to write. Most days he would get out of bed early, leaving Geraldine fast asleep, and creep into his study and begin. He liked the dawn chorus which inspired him and gave him ideas. Some days he didn't have a clue what he was going to write until he heard a little bird chirping outside. He wondered if it was the same one each morning. He'd open the window a bit so he could hear it more clearly, even though it was now seasonally cold. It was worth it as the bird responded and seemed to magnify its chorus leaving Jim lost, absorbing such grace. After that words would briskly flow out of him onto the page.

When environmental or political issues arose, he felt that he had to write about them, get them down on paper and firmly out of his system. Certain things would stimulate his writing like the George Floyd incident in Minneapolis. He felt so angry that atrocities like this could still happen in this day and age. Sometimes he wondered what he would do if he didn't have his writing. At other times he wished he'd begun years ago, thus lessening the frustration that had built up.

The more he wrote, the more he questioned how civilisation worked and produced harmony. Surely it didn't matter what colour people were or where they came from. This had to be the most basic principle that everyone lived by, otherwise how could humanity grow and develop?

Jim took out his poem for the Positive Images competition one morning and began editing it. Neighbourhoods were more important than ever this year with the lockdown and people were understandably keeping more of an eye on elderly people living alone. Loneliness was something people hadn't talked about much before because of its obvious stigma, but it had now come to the forefront. People were talking to each other over their garden fences like they used to when Jim was growing up, and they even sat out front some days which he'd never seen before.

Jim read and reread his poem several times. When he read it aloud, he felt it had a good beat and was happy with it. He had written about his neighbours as a child growing up and then as an adult several years later; how things had changed in some ways, but not in others. There were a few familiar faces, but most had moved on or passed away. The spirit of the neighbourhood remained though, and his poem concluded it always would.

It was very personal to Jim and he initially felt reluctant to show it to anyone. Then he built up the courage to show it to Geraldine who was quite emotional after reading it.

"That's lovely," she said.

"Do you think so?" questioned Jim.

"I certainly do, and the other poets will like it as well when you read it next week."

Chapter 12 – The City of Culture

Coventry was to be the City of Culture next year and events were being planned despite the current lockdown in the belief it would happen even if a little late. Everyone knew that there were pockets of culture around the city, but Jim and Geraldine and many others thought it would be good bringing them all together under one celebratory umbrella. Jim had Scottish parents and Geraldine's were Irish and they were brought up respectively in these cultures. They were proud of their roots as well as the city where they now lived, like many people from around the world who had made Coventry their home. Immigrants had brought their pride with them from their country of origin and such fulfilment permeated their homes and would be passed on to future generations.

Both Jim and Geraldine knew that Coventry had been a major manufacturing hub for centuries, producing dyes, leather products, cloth, ribbons and watches. The silk trade, especially, had been here since the 17th century – originally woven on handlooms in people's houses. More recently, Coventry was the birthplace of the mass-produced modern bicycle, then motor vehicles for decades. After the devastation of the city during the Second World War, its whole infrastructure had to be rebuilt throughout the second half of the 20th century. This attracted new people to the city which resulted in a woven tapestry of different cultures.

Geraldine was aware of what refugees and migrants brought to the city, having worked with them in an advice centre. She was proud of the fact that many people had arrived from places like Syria, Afghanistan and Iran in order to make Coventry their new home, and that her city had more Syrian refugees per capita than any other in the UK. The city was constantly changing as people from all over the world settled here.

"People take their culture with them wherever they go. In fact, they hang on to it more when they leave their homeplace. The culture here is getting richer and richer."

"It was like that with my parents always celebrating Burns Night," replied Jim.

"Mine too celebrating St Patrick's Day, with shamrock being flown over from Ireland for the special day," said Geraldine.

"When I was younger and lived with my parents, a Chinese family next door used to give us red envelopes when it was the Chinese New Year."

"We all want to keep hold of something that our forefathers did. I suppose it's natural really. But I think it's beautiful when all the cultures come together, showing off their colours and different attire."

"They're then seen as a greater whole rather than separate factions."

"That's what I'm hoping the City of Culture will bring us."

"What about the music scene in this city?" asked Jim.

"I was really into Two-tone music in my early days and liked The Specials and The Selecter."

"I hear there's going to be an exhibition at the Herbert."

"That's right. It's going to be the first ever major exhibition in the UK solely devoted to the Two-tone music scene."

"Yes, Two-tone originated in the 70s with Coventry's thriving music scene."

"They were trying to diffuse racial tensions in Britain at that time, but there are still racial problems today. Some things haven't changed at all."

"Do you know any famous writers from this city?"

"Yes, sure - Philip Larkin and George Eliot. There's also Lee Child. I've read some of his books."

"What about Debbie Isitt, the screenwriter and producer of the Nativity films."

"Yeah, I didn't think about her."

"And the up-and-coming poet, Jim McClean."

"I wish I was that good, but haven't been writing long enough."

"You wait until you get your poems published."

"Thank you," said Jim, as he took hold of her hands and gently kissed her on the top of her head. "I don't know what I'd do without all your encouragement."

The two of them were quiet for a while, just enjoying each other's company. They often found themselves like this and didn't mind the quietness they shared.

"Talking of different cultures," Jim said, after a while, "I was thinking about the allotment and what we could grow next year. I could plant some exotic vegetable seeds and edible flowers for salads, and see how the soil takes to them."

"That's a good idea - see how they grow. That's how you learn, and you may be quite surprised, especially with your greenhouse starting them off."

"OK. I'll look into it more and check what seeds I can get online."

Winter

Chapter 13 - Rest

Jim's dad had been fascinated with nature. He admired how swallows would simply flow with the seasons when the temperature began to fall and how they gathered on telephone wires chattering away, preparing for their journey south. He loved seeing them return in April or May and felt in some way that they belonged to him or were a part of him. He would take Jim out for walks in the woods near their home, and Jim remembered how excited his dad got when they heard the first cuckoo of spring. He beamed like a child as if it was the first time he'd ever heard it.

Hibernation in winter was the side of nature that Jim's dad admired the most and Jim often wondered as a child how the animals knew when to hibernate.

"They just do," his dad said, when he asked him one day. "They have to rest in the winter months so they're full of zest when it becomes warmer again. It's how they survive, and we should do the same. We all need rest."

Jim would ponder this for a while and then ask, "Are we like the animals then?"

"We are, son, and the more you look into nature, the more you will see it."

Jim couldn't get this into his head and would just go back to looking through his football sticker album that he'd almost completed.

Such sentiment, however, never left Jim entirely. And it was often when at raves and on drugs in his late teens that his dad's words came back to him. He knew he was living on the edge, needed rest and couldn't continue like this. And, although he enjoyed the thrill of raves and drugs, deep down he wasn't happy. "We all need rest" were the words that kept haunting him.

Jim's dad was adamant about turning the soil at the allotment and leaving that to rest too over the winter. It's what his father taught him in Scotland whilst he was growing up.

"The soil needs rest, just like us," he would say. "It can't work throughout the year non-stop. Its goodness will just fade away when it should be regenerating itself. If it doesn't, there'll be nothing left for future generations."

Jim had been thinking this when he last went down to the allotment and was digging up the soil to let it rest over the winter months. These are the simple principles which we have to adhere to, he thought, and bring into most areas of our lives. But there are so many distractions nowadays and that's why we find it hard to relax and rest as we should.

This winter Jim was going to try and relax more, and store up his energy so he would be ready for the spring and the new ventures that such a season brought. He was now in a relationship with somebody he loved and wanted to share his life with.

Geraldine slept in now that the mornings were darker. Jim noticed her effortlessly adapting to the new season, doing less but also eating wholesome, nutritious food. The house smelled so much better now Geraldine had moved in. Jim liked the aroma from her cooking, but most of all he loved Geraldine's scent which never seemed to leave him.

Jim tried altering his writing pattern now that the winter months were here. Rather than getting up early in the morning darkness, he tried writing in the evenings. It didn't work though as he'd be thinking about what he'd done during the day and the conversations he'd had with Geraldine. He found it hard to concentrate as he had managed to do earlier in the year – feeling fresh upon waking. He tried writing in the middle of the day therefore, but this didn't work too well either as he'd be thinking about his evening meal and how nice it was sitting opposite someone now he had a partner.

"Why don't you give it a rest for the winter?" said Geraldine, as they sat down at lunch together to have some vegetable soup one day.

"What? The writing?"

"Yes. Give it a rest. It'll do you good."

"Really?"

"Yes - really. Do something different for a while. Then, when you go back to it, you'll see things from another perspective."

"So, give the writing a rest, like soil in the winter?"

"Now you're getting it," Geraldine laughed, as she wrapped her arms tightly around his waist.

Chapter 14 – Second Lockdown

Jim and Geraldine were on the settee with their arms around each other in front of the fire that was burning brightly. Jim liked preparing the fire as his dad used to. As a child he would sit on the rug in front of the fire and watch the flames flicker with fascination while his parents sat behind him admiringly. His dad would dim the lights so they could see the shadows of the flames on the wall. They wouldn't talk much - just the odd word to one another. After a while, Jim would curl up and fall asleep with his back to the fire, and Jim's dad would lift him up and carry him to bed.

Jim was now going through his old record collection, trying to sort them into some kind of order, while Geraldine had her feet up on the settee reading a book; her bandana beside her as she'd not long come back from the shops. The house felt more like their own after the work they'd done on it. And it was like they'd been together for a very long time. They were so relaxed in each other's company and, despite the lockdown, it felt like a new horizon was stretching out before them.

"I'm beginning to like this lockdown," said Jim. "It takes the pressure off and you can just do your own thing. I miss going to The Plough though."

"Me too – especially on Sundays. I love their vegetarian lunch," replied Geraldine.

"Yes, I suppose it's the things we took for granted that we miss."

"I know. And this is the second one. How long do you think it will last?"

"I don't know. They're saying it will ease off before Christmas, but I can't see how that will happen with infection rates on the rise again."

"The announcement of the second lockdown certainly came on the right day if the Government is trying to scare us."

"Why?"

"It was on Halloween. A scriptwriter couldn't have timed it better."

"You're right. People are going to look back in years to come at this period and not believe how it was handled. Before this second lockdown we had places in different tiers which meant if you lived in Tier 3 you couldn't go out for a drink as pubs were closed, but you could travel a short distance to a Tier 2 location and order a swift pint! Also, pubs closing early and everyone leaving together - surely the virus loved that. I know it's coming up to panto season, but you couldn't make this up."

"It's the fear the Government is instilling that's the main problem. People are afraid to go out or visit loved ones, and elderly people are left all alone. If my parents were alive, I wouldn't have stopped seeing them."

"They say that mental health problems are rising due to all this isolation. Winter is a hard enough time anyway even without all this going on."

"My friend works as a mental health nurse and she says that the insecurity caused by the pandemic is increasing mental health problems for people of all ages."

"It could end up being worse than the actual Coronavirus."

"It will, Jim, and it'll have long-term effects."

Jim reached over and took hold of Geraldine's hand which was warm from the fire he'd lit earlier. They now needed each other more than ever. It was the doubt that everyone was feeling during these strange times that made having someone beside you to talk to and comfort you invaluable.

"Oh, I've been meaning to tell you that I've applied for seasonal, part-time work at Sainsbury's," said Jim. "They're taking on people during the Christmas period and I've got an interview next week."

"That's great news. You'll meet lots of interesting people there from all walks of life - both staff and the public."

"That's what I thought. And not many other places are open. It's going to be a different Christmas for sure."

"It certainly is. But you'll get ideas working at a supermarket for your writing from the people you meet and talk to. You can build up a dossier of characters in your mind. I used to work at Lidl, and you'd be amazed at the ideas I got for my artwork while working there. The mind sometimes goes off to a special place when you're doing ordinary work, which helps creative types like us."

"It's a bit of a downgrade from the accountancy job I had in the city, but it's just a few shifts a week and I think I'll enjoy meeting people."

"You will and you won't regret it. And I'm sure people will like your Scottish charm."

"Yes, maybe," laughed Jim.

Chapter 15 – Lockdown Christmas

Jim was going to the allotment once or twice a week to dig up the root vegetables and noticed that the Brussels sprouts were now ready. He remembered his dad saying how root vegetables liked frost because it made them sweeter. Well, there wasn't much frost this year with temperatures in December higher than normal, Jim thought. It was 13 degrees on the winter solstice and felt like a spring day when Jim and Geraldine strolled along the river bank in the park. They sat on a bench by a huge oak tree at the top of the hill and both thought that something wasn't right. Normally they would be wrapped up at this time of year.

"It'll be one of the warmest years on record," said Jim, as they sat holding hands.

"Yes, it will be. I was reading that the top ten warmest years on record have been since 2002."

"There's no doubt about it - the Earth is warming up."

"That's why we have to do something. We have lots of plans for next year with the G7 Summit in Cornwall and COP26 in Glasgow. We're offering sessions online informing and educating people about the state of the world - how we're reaching the tipping point and what we can do to avert such a tragedy. This is our opportunity for major change."

"It's a matter of letting people know what's really going on that's important. Once they know, they'll hopefully do something about it. That's what I like about the Citizens' Assembly - it gives power to ordinary people to make decisions about real things that affect their lives, their future and generations to come."

"That's right - power back to the people."

Jim and Geraldine walked back alongside the river, still holding hands. They were going to spend their first Christmas together and it would be extra special this year with no places to go or people to visit - instead, just the two of them. It had been a long time since either had been in a relationship and they were simply enjoying the company of each other.

They slowed down as they passed by the meadow, admiring the wildflowers and their changing colours throughout the seasons. The pond had attracted a variety of insects, bathing birds, damselflies and dragonflies; the latter laying their eggs during the summer.

Jim had started his job at Sainsbury's working three shifts a week. He met many old faces that he'd not seen for a long time and was amazed at the mixture of people working there – even former executives who'd lost their jobs and were now working as delivery drivers.

"The public appreciate what we're doing during this pandemic with most other places closed," Jim said to Geraldine one evening over dinner after returning from a shift. "We've even been called the forgotten key workers and there have been cards and chocolates from customers thanking us for the work we're doing. Some people go to the supermarket for a family outing as there is nowhere else to go!"

"What kind of work are you doing?"

"All sorts - stacking shelves, working on the till and helping with customer queries."

"And are you getting any writing ideas?"

"Loads. I'm planning a short story about the role of a store detective. I'm looking forward to writing it and have already made some notes."

"That's brilliant," said Geraldine.

"It's you I've got to thank," he said, as he leaned over the table and kissed her.

~ ~ ~

The temperature dropped on Christmas Eve and it instantly felt more normal to Jim and Geraldine. They had put decorations up and a Christmas tree they'd bought from a local farm. The fire was lit, and it felt very special to them as they hadn't experienced such festive togetherness for a long time. Jim still missed his dad and the memorable time they'd had together when he came back from London, but he felt better knowing that both his parents had, at different times, known Geraldine.

It was like a new house, not just because of the Christmas decorations, but due to the painting they had done. Each room felt clean and fresh and they'd had a big clear out before putting up the curtains Geraldine had made.

They were busy Christmas morning preparing the dinner. They enjoyed such activities together, particularly using vegetables from their allotments. They both felt there was something unique about cooking their own produce which they'd planted as seed many months ago and helped to grow and mature. And they'd left some of their vegetables on their neighbours' doorsteps in the run up to Christmas as they had plenty to spare.

The house was full of cooking aromas, and the old table that Jim had used to write on during the year had been brought into the living room, now laid out for the two of them. Everything felt just right.

The presents they got each other weren't big and expensive, but items they thought would be meaningful. Geraldine's main gift to Jim was a book on how to grow vegetables organically, which he appreciated as he still had much to learn. Jim bought Geraldine a Celtic Knot necklace which she liked very much and immediately put on.

They talked a lot about their earlier lives - jobs they'd had, relationships that didn't work out and people they knew. They felt that they could just pour out their thoughts which was refreshing for both of them. Geraldine had spent many years abroad working as an English teacher and was engaged to be married until her partner went off with another woman and she returned home broken-hearted.

After dinner Jim and Geraldine contacted some of their friends by telephone and on Zoom to see how they were getting on during this lockdown Christmas. They wished them well, particularly those who were alone or not allowed to travel; some isolating as they had tested positive. It was the strangest Christmas people had ever experienced. There was a quietness about the city though that many folks liked. This was how Christmases perhaps used to be, thought Jim – less grand, but still beautiful.

Jim and Geraldine felt that they were making a new start. There seemed to be possibilities ahead of them and exciting opportunities, especially with the City of Culture about to happen. Although there was nowhere to go and no one to see, they both felt quietly excited and patient, like seeds in the ground, over where their new love would take them.

Chapter 16 – The North Star

Jim and Geraldine were looking forward to returning to The Plough on Sunday afternoons once the lockdown was lifted, although they weren't too sure when that would be. They missed the landlady and people who went there regularly. There was one old man who used to sit in the corner drinking his pint slowly who they'd have the odd word with. They wished they knew where he lived so they could check up on him to see if he was alright. They worried about certain people and often phoned them for a chat to see how they were getting on. Most were OK and some living alone were occasionally faring better than families; households juggling working from home and managing their children's online learning.

With cinemas, restaurants and forms of entertainment closed, Jim and Geraldine decided to join an online sea shanty singing group. They enjoyed it immensely and liked the mix of people they mingled with. Singing during lockdown was a good tonic for the two of them and old fishing songs - originally sung by sailors - felt appropriate in getting them through troubled waters. They reminded Jim of the singalongs with his family as a child when they went on holiday to the Isle of Arran.

Jim was planning to return to his writing in the New Year as his seasonal work at Sainsbury's would be finishing around then. Having a break from writing wasn't a bad idea, as Geraldine had said. In fact, they were talking the other day about how all art forms have their peaks and troughs, just like the seasons.

"I'm going to concentrate more on short stories now, I think," said Jim one morning, as they were getting ready to go out for a walk.

"That's a good idea," replied Geraldine. "You can write what you want. And be your own master of ceremony."

"That's the funny thing about writing. It just seems to take off sometimes, meaning all I need to do is keep hold of the steering wheel."

"I like that," said Geraldine. "You've found your raison d'être."

"I feel something new is coming to us all. We have the threat of the Coronavirus pandemic and climate emergency, but with that a new wave of energy. I'm not sure how to chronicle it, but it's somehow bringing people together and is very real."

"I know. I can feel it too."

Jim admired how his parents had gently flowed through the seasons of life, accepting what came their way. He often wondered how they would have coped with the fear of getting Coronavirus, plus their reaction to the lockdown. But then he imagined they would have just taken it in their stride, adapting where necessary - using common sense and thinking more about others than themselves. This was the path they had shown Jim, and he now felt he had a purpose and was heading in the right direction. It was like he had gone full circle and was starting again.

Jim and Geraldine would go for walks with Theo in the mornings and late afternoons, through the allotments and into the park by the meadow. The quietness and stillness seemed to echo centuries gone by; nobody rushing about; the dormancy of the Earth almost able to be heard as they sauntered along during the Christmas lockdown week.

They were soul mates, now joined. The whole universe is happy for us, thought Jim, as he looked up at the darkening sky one evening and saw the stars coming out. He stood there for a while, holding Geraldine's hand, gazing at the full moon whilst locating the Plough and then the North Star. It was shining brightly – Polaris, as it was known - as Jim contemplated its presence and immediately thought...our paths were already set. He gave it a brief nod, before walking on with Geraldine by the flowing river.

THE END

Printed in Great Britain
by Amazon

19274807R00068